Little Robot Alone

BY Patricia MacLachlan AND Emily MacLachlan Charest

ILLUSTRATED BY Matt Phelan

Houghton Mifflin Harcourt
Boston   New York

Little Robot lived in a white house
on a green hill by a blue pond.

Every morning he put on his tracks.

*One by one, tight and strong,
rolling, strolling, all day long.*

He charged his battery.

*Zippity zappity,
Crickety crackety,
Hum Hum Hum.*

And he sang his cheerful breakfast song.

Oats with oozy oil are yummy,
slipping slowly down my tummy.

Little Robot had a peaceful life.
He watched the birds fly over his white house.
He watched the squirrels race on the green hill.
He watched the fish splash in the blue pond.

But he felt alone.

One night Little Robot dreamed of a smooth, shiny shape.

When he woke in the morning,
he had an idea!

First he put on his tracks.

One by one, tight and strong,
rolling, strolling, all day long.

He charged his battery.

Zippity zappity,
Crickity crackety,
Hum Hum Hum.

He sang his cheerful breakfast song.

Oats with oozy oil are yummy,
slipping slowly down my tummy.

Then Little Robot began.

Here's my bag. An oily rag.
Pegs, glue, where are you?
Battery, screws, a handy wrench.
I'll put them all upon my bench.

Little Robot bent the metal into a shape.
He used a screwdriver to attach the ends.
He worked,
and worked,
and WORKED!

Finally, on his bench was something smooth and shiny.
It had four wooden legs and a button.
Little Robot pressed the button.
Nothing.

Little Robot pressed the button again.
Nothing.
Little Robot thought hard.
He had more to do.

He rolled to his bag of treasures.
He found two bright marbles,

some soft wool,

and a small broom.

Then he worked,
and worked,
and WORKED!

Little Robot took a deep breath.
He added tracks and squirted them with oil.

One by one, tight and strong,
rolling, strolling, all day long.

He charged the battery.

Zippity zappity,
Crickity crackety,
Hum Hum Hum.

His new thing shook!
The broom wagged!
Little Robot jumped back.

He pressed the button.

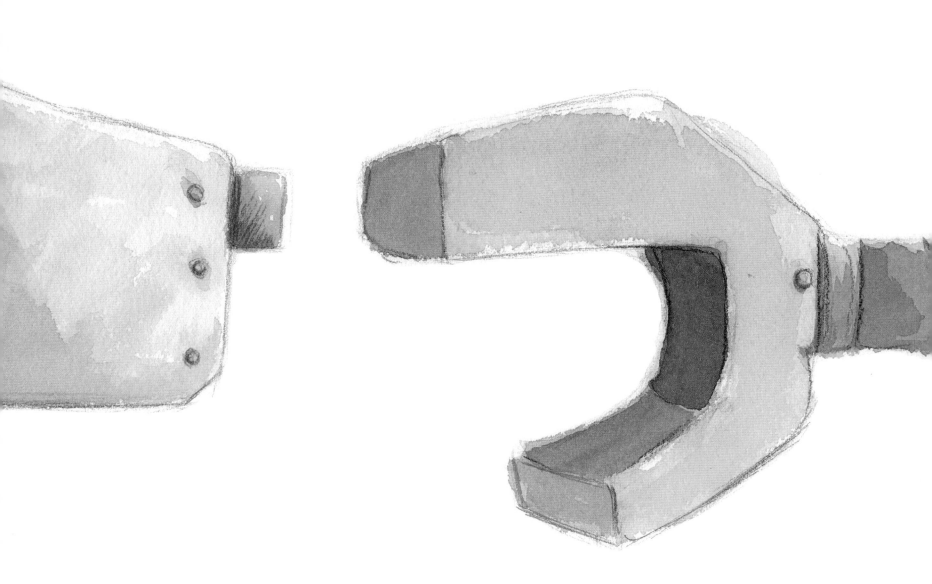

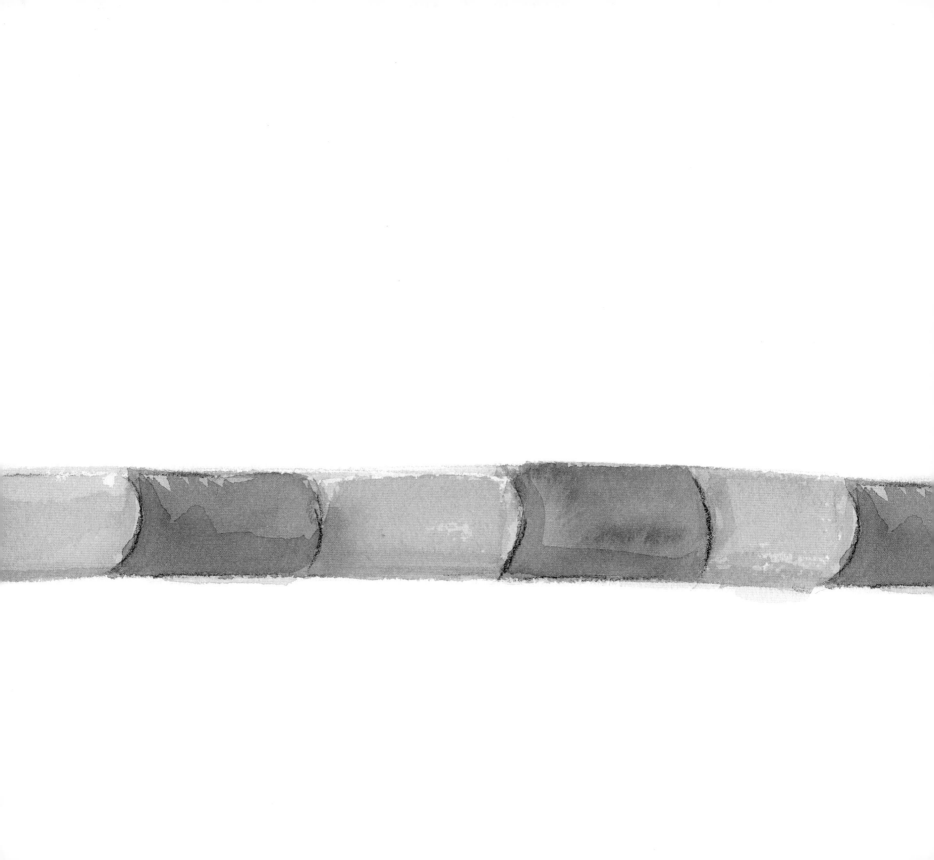

And his new thing leaned over
and licked Little Robot
on his smooth metal cheek.

"Can you talk?" asked Little Robot softly.
"Woof," it said.

Little Robot reached out
and patted the smooth, shiny body.
"Welcome home," he whispered, "my friend."

Little Robot rolled outside.
"Little Dog is here!" he called out.
The birds flew down to see.
The squirrels on the green hill came close.
The fish in the blue pond had a look.

Little Dog sniffed the air.
He watched the birds.
He wagged his broom tail
at the squirrels and the fish.

As the stars came out,
Little Robot and Little Dog
rolled into their white house
and under a moonlit quilt.

"Good night, Little Dog,"
whispered Little Robot.
His friend was already asleep.

Sleep happy, sleep well,
until the night's end,
my good Little Dog,
my good little friend.

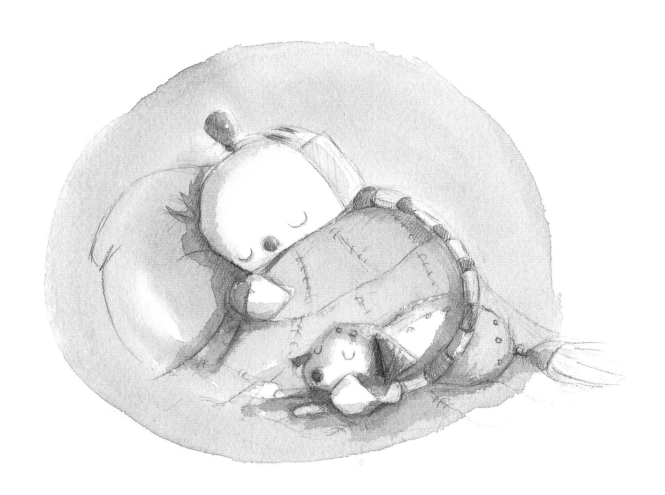

For Dean and his robots —Love Patty and Emily

For Nora and Jasper —Matt

Text copyright © 2018 by Patricia MacLachlan and Emily MacLachlan Charest • Illustrations copyright © 2018 by Matt Phelan
All rights reserved. For information about permission to reproduce selections from this book, write to trade.permissions@hmhco.com
or to Permissions, Houghton Mifflin Harcourt Publishing Company, 3 Park Avenue, 19th Floor, New York, New York 10016. • hmhco.com
The illustrations in this book were done in pencil and watercolor on Arches cold-pressed paper.
The text type was set in Aged. • The display type was set in ArcherPro.
Library of Congress Cataloging-in-Publication Data is on file. • ISBN 978-0-544-44280-1
Manufactured in China • SCP 10 9 8 7 6 5 4 3 2 1 • 4500698465